Rob at S

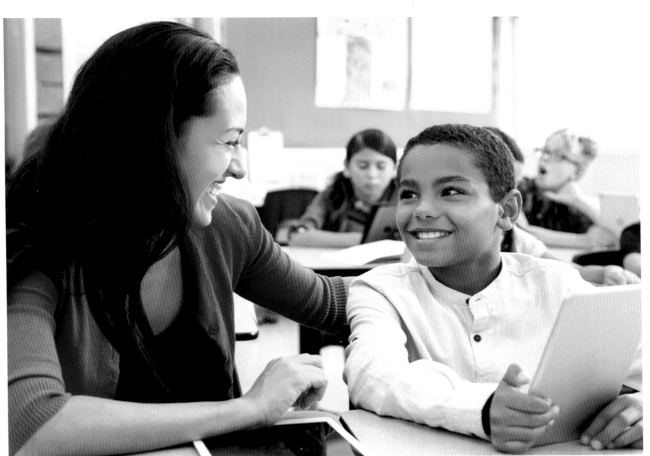

by Rachel Rosen

It is a 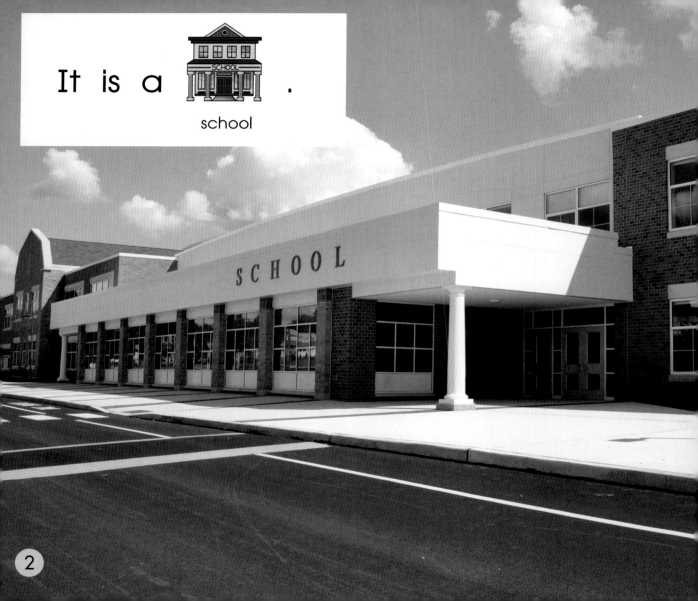 .

school

It has a big 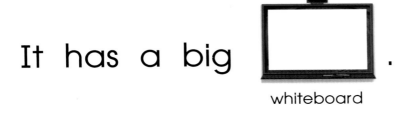 .

whiteboard

Rob can tap on 2.

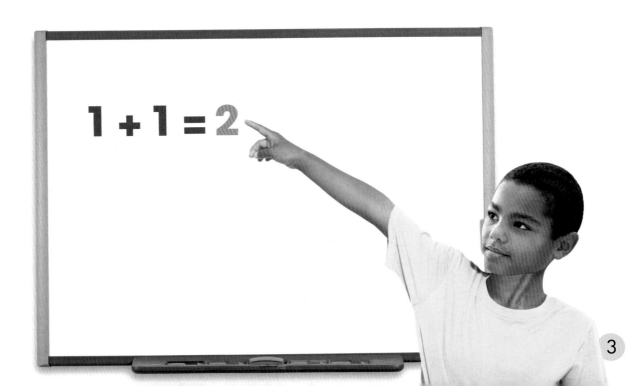

$$1 + 1 = 2$$

It is a 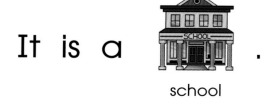 .

school

It has 4 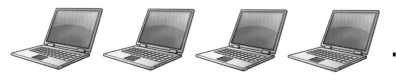 .

computers

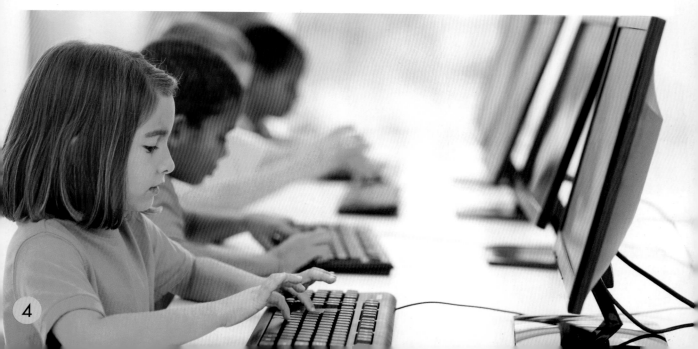

Ron can see a 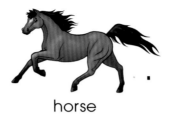.

horse

The 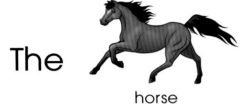 can run and run.

horse

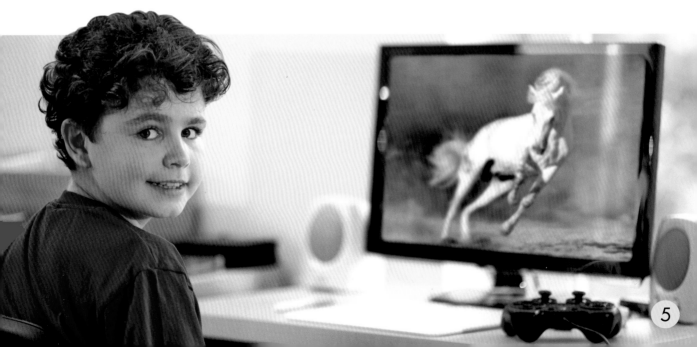

It is a 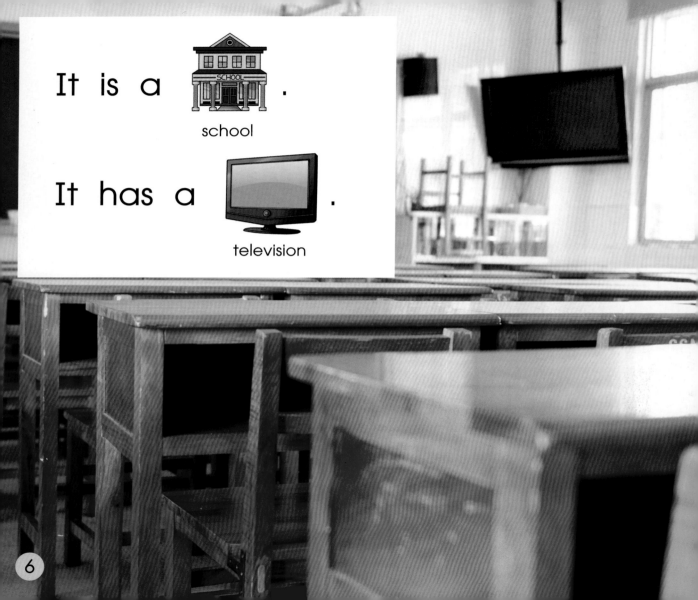 .

school

It has a .

television

I can see a rib.

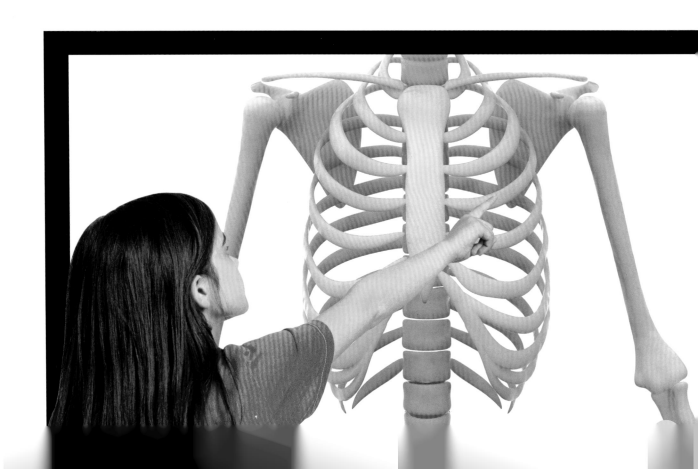

I like 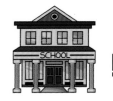 !

school

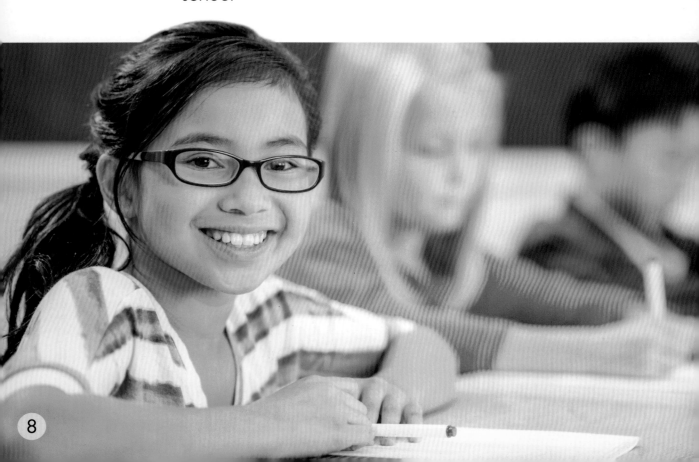